the Apple Pie that Papa Baked

By Lauren Thompson

Illustrated by Jonathan Bean

Simon & Schuster Books for Young Readers
New York   London   Toronto   Sydney

A note from the illustrator about the art:

Each illustration is made up of three separate drawings—done on separate sheets
of vellum paper—for each of the colors (red, yellow, and black). As I am drawing, I can tell
how the separate drawings will look together because vellum is semitranslucent and I can see
the drawings beneath as I work on the top drawing. All the drawings are done in black ink
and only receive their color when I scan them separately into my computer, recompose the
images, and assign each drawing its proper color (red, yellow, or black)!

SIMON & SCHUSTER BOOKS FOR YOUNG READERS
An imprint of Simon & Schuster Children's Publishing Division
1230 Avenue of the Americas, New York, New York 10020
Text copyright © 2007 by Lauren Thompson
Illustrations copyright © 2007 by Jonathan Bean
All rights reserved, including the right of reproduction in whole or in part in any form.
SIMON & SCHUSTER BOOKS FOR YOUNG READERS is a trademark of Simon & Schuster, Inc.
Book design by Lizzy Bromley
The text for this book is set in Letterpress Text.
Manufactured in China
2 4 6 8 10 9 7 5 3 1
CIP data for this book is available from the Library of Congress.
ISBN-13: 978-1-4169-1240-8
ISBN-10: 1-4169-1240-1

first·
edition

For Robert, who loves pie
—L. T.

To my father and his orchard
—J. B.

This is the pie, warm and sweet,
that Papa baked.

These are the **apples**, juicy and red,

that went in the pie, warm and sweet,
that Papa baked.

This is the tree, crooked and strong,

that grew the apples, juicy and red,
that went in the pie, warm and sweet,
that Papa baked.

These are the **roots**, deep and fine,

that fed the tree, crooked and strong,
that grew the apples, juicy and red,
that went in the pie, warm and sweet,
that Papa baked.

This is the **rain**, cool and fresh,

that watered the roots, deep and fine,
that fed the tree, crooked and strong,
that grew the apples, juicy and red,
that went in the pie, warm and sweet,
that Papa baked.

These are the **clouds**,
    heaped and round,

that dropped the rain,
    cool and fresh,
that watered the roots,
    deep and fine,
that fed the tree,
    crooked and strong,

that grew the apples, juicy and red,
that went in the pie, warm and sweet,
that Papa baked.

This is the sky,
    wide and fair,

that carried the clouds,
    heaped and round,
that dropped the rain,
    cool and fresh,
that watered the roots,
    deep and fine,
that fed the tree,
    crooked and strong,
that grew the apples,
    juicy and red,
that went in the pie,
    warm and sweet,
that Papa baked.

This is the **sun**, fiery and bright,

that lit the sky,
　　wide and fair,
that carried the clouds,
　　heaped and round,
that dropped the rain,
　　cool and fresh,
that watered the roots,
　　deep and fine,
that fed the tree,
　　crooked and strong,
that grew the apples,
　　juicy and red,
that went in the pie,
　　warm and sweet,
that Papa baked.

This is the **world**,
blooming with life,

that spins with the sun, fiery and bright,
that lights the sky, wide and fair,
that carries the clouds, heaped and round,
that drops the rain, cool and fresh,

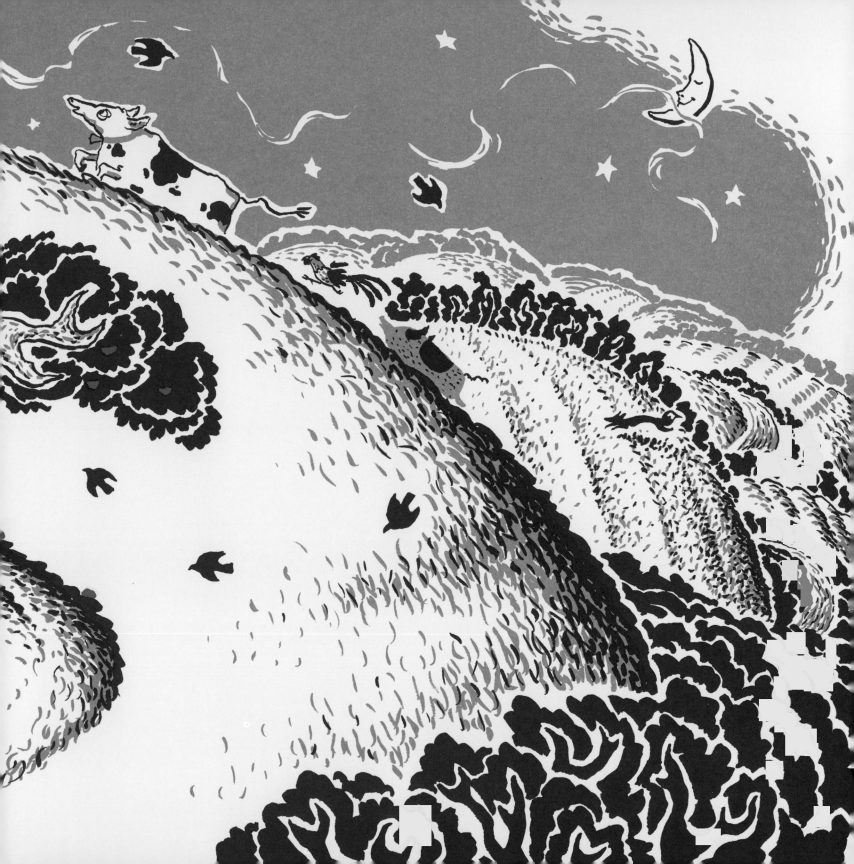

that waters the roots, deep and fine,
that feed the tree, crooked and strong,
that grows the apples, juicy and red,
that go in the pies, warm and sweet,
that Papa bakes.

This is the pie, warm and sweet,
that Papa baked . . .

. . . and for you!

The End